My X Y Z Book

by Jane Belk Moncure

illustrated by Linda Hohag

Library of Congress Cataloging in Publication Data

Moncure, Jane Belk.
  My "xyz" book.

  (My first steps to reading)
  Rev. ed. of: My x, y, z sound box. © 1979.
  Summary: Little x, Little y, and Little z fill
their boxes with things that begin with the letters
x, y, and z.
  1. Children's stories, American. [1. Alphabet]
I. Hohag, Linda. ill. II. Moncure, Jane Belk. My
x, y, z, sound box. III. Title. IV. Series: Moncure,
Jane Belk. My first steps to reading.
PZ7.M739Myx 1984   [E]   84-17561
ISBN 0-89565-295-1

Distributed by Childrens Press, 5440 North Cumberland Avenue,
Chicago, Illinois 60656

My "x, y, z" Book

Little  had a box.

6

He said, "I will fill my  box."

Little found an

x-ray machine.

"Excellent," said Little .

"With my x-ray machine,

I can see inside of things."

He made
an x-ray of
his hands.

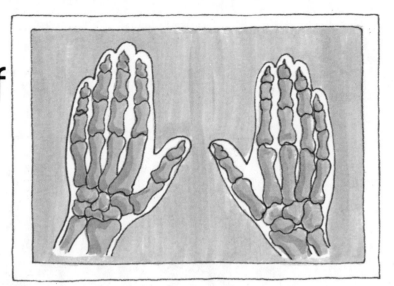

He could see his bones.
"Excellent," he said.

He put the x-ray picture
into his 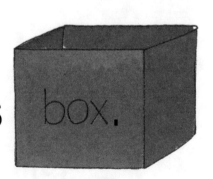 box.

He made an x-ray of his feet.

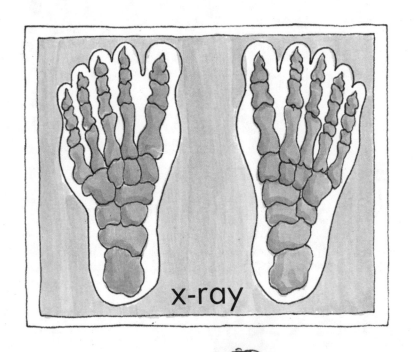

x-ray

"Excellent," Little said. "I can see the bones in my feet."

Then he put the
x-ray picture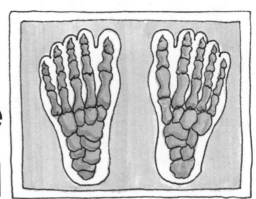
and
the x-ray machine

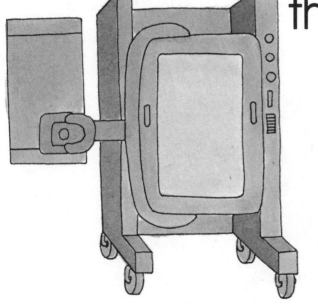

into his

He said, "Now I will
call my friend…

Little . He may have a box."

"I do," said Little .

"I will fill my box too."

Little Y found a yo-yo.

It was a yellow yo-yo.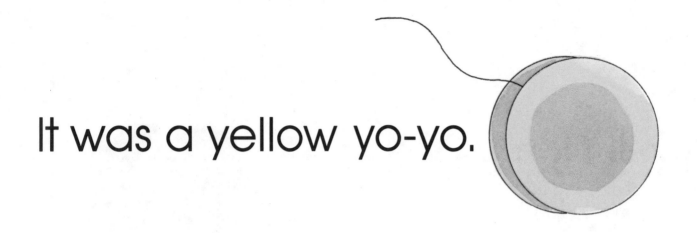

He tried to make the
yo-yo go up

and
down.

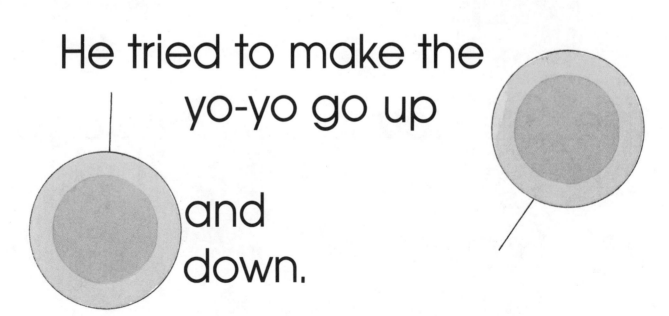

But the string was too short.

Little found yarn.

He tied the yarn
to the yo-yo string.

Now the yo-yo went

down

and up,

down

and up.

Little  turned the box upside down.

He stood on the box.
His yo-yo went way down, and way up.

He said, "I will call my friend...

17

Little  and see if she

has a  box."

"I do," said Little .

"I will fill my box, too."

She found a zebra...

and two
more zebras.

Little  found three zebras,

one,

two,

three.

"In you go," she said.

But the zebras jumped
out of the box, zip, zip.

Away they ran,
zig-zag

down the road.

Guess who ran after them?

Guess where they went?

They went to
the zoo.

More about Little .

Sometimes "x" sounds like "z." as in these words. Read them.

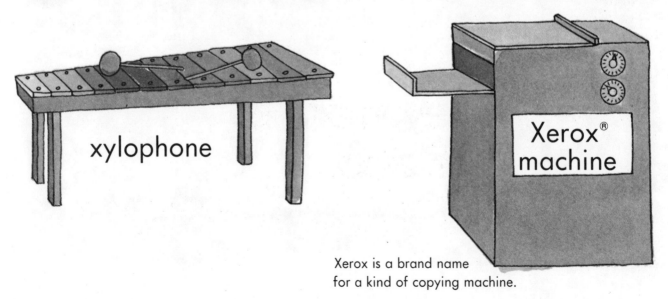

xylophone

Xerox® machine

Xerox is a brand name for a kind of copying machine.

More words with Little .

yams

yacht

yard

yak

29

More words with Little 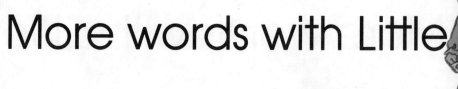.

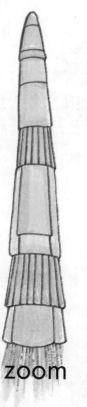

zoom

zipper

zinnia

zero

O1 2 3